Brave
Little Ones

BRAVE LITTLE ONES
Copyright © 2018 by George Zelina
Illustrated by Henriett Maczó

Copyright © 2018 Brave Little Ones

Brave Little Ones

WRITTEN BY GEORGE ZELINA

ILLUSTRATED BY HENRIETT MACZÓ

Table of Contents

Charlie
The Guardian of the Ducks

Charlie had a passion for superheroes. He talked about them all the time, to anyone who would listen. He talked about superheroes to his friends and, of course, he talked about superheroes to his parents. He talked about how he wanted to meet a superhero. And he talked about how he wanted to *be* a superhero. Of all the people Charlie talked about superheroes with, his mom and dad were the ones who cared the most about what he had to say.

Not too long ago, on his fifth birthday, Charlie's mom and dad gave him a bright green cape, a black velvet mask, and an extendable plastic stick. The stick looked like a magic wand. Charlie knew then, that one day he would become a superhero. He would be the greatest superhero of them all! There are a lot of children, adults, and animals who need superheroes, Charlie reflected. He also told himself that with lots and lots of practice and perseverance, one day he will come to their rescue.

Every night, while watching cartoons, Charlie put on his mysterious superhero outfit and followed along, mirroring the movements of his favorite heroes.
He worried with them and laughed with them. He spun his magic wand. Soon he was doing it with a little bit of flash and a lot of polish. And that wasn't a surprise, because Charlie was practicing every day and every night.

One evening, just before going to bed, while Charlie was brushing his teeth, he heard a strange noise come through the windows of the bathroom.

Pimbadabumm. Pimpadabumm. Pimbadabumm. The sound was rhythmic, and it ended in a dull thud that came from somewhere near their house. Charlie poked his head around the corner to talk to his parents.

"Mom, Dad, what's that strange noise?"

"I think it's just the birds having a falling out with each other at the bird feeder." his dad replied, while he put back his toothbrush in its place.

"Yes, yes, it's probably that." agreed his mother.

But Charlie couldn't let the matter rest. He could have sworn he had heard the noise before. As Dad was sitting on the edge of his bed reading a bedtime story, Charlie gave a hiss.

"Dad! Dad! I know what the noise was." he said in a burst of excitement.
"So, what was it, son?"

"Do you remember last year when the little ducklings waddled up here from the lake at the end of the road? Everyone was worrying about how they would find their way back to their mother?" Charlie asked. If was obvious from the tone of his voice that he was worried.

"Yes, I remember. We had to catch them and bring them all back down the lake. It took a long time," his dad said, recalling the episode.

"I heard the same noise last year. It was because the ducklings got on top of the porch and were waddling around. Dad, you have to check! Please!" Charlie was practically shouting.

His dad stood up. "I'll go and check it out." he said. "If it makes you feel better."

9

While his dad was outside, Charlie began to pace his room. And as he paced he thought about what he had to do.

Taking the ducklings back to their mother? Now this is a real job for a superhero!

Charlie practically jumped out of his pajamas. He put on a t-shirt, a warm sweater, pants, and a pair of warm socks. Then he put on his bright green cape, throwing it over his shoulder with a flourish, and his black velvet mask. Finally, he took out his expandable stick.

Mom and Dad were standing at the entrance door. They were both furrowing their brows and scratching their heads. Charlie was right! The little ducklings were wandering around and jumping on the porch. Some of them were chirping and crying. They were upset because they were looking for their mother and their mother was nowhere to be found.

"Poor ducklings. How will they get back to their mother?" his mom asked.

"Don't worry Mom! Don't worry Dad! This is a job for

Charlie! The Guardian of the Ducks!" Charlie shouted with gusto.

They turned around and there he stood; Charlie, the Guardian of the Ducks, in all his glory. His beautiful green cape was fluttering in the wind. Even behind his black velvet mask, his glowing, determined look could be seen. And there was something on the end of the stick. Ducky, the small plush duck, which has been resting on the bottom of the toy box for months. Charlie had tied the stuffed animal duck on the end of his stick. He had truly become the Guardian of the Ducks.

"Madam and sir! Put on a coat because it's cold and do come with me!" said Charlie, the Guardian of the Ducks.

The parents didn't say anything. Charlie's forthright manner was so impressive they just did what he asked. On the porch, there were ten snowball sized gold-colored little ducks quacking and waddling in a confused jumble. They kept bumping against each other and they were turning back and forth. It was a funny sight to see, but Charlie knew they were missing their mother and would only get more and more frightened. He had to get to work.

"Listen up, ducks! Now you do what I say! Here's Ducky, your tour guide." Here Charlie made a wide wave in the air with the duck-tipped magic wand. "Watch and follow Ducky!" He gave the stick a good hard shake.

The little ducklings all stopped and stared. Every one of them stopped waddling and focused their eyes on Ducky. Charlie, the Guardian of the Ducks headed out and Dad, Mom and the 10 ducklings marched after him as one team, towards the lake.

They walked past the road, down a trail full of cats, and past dangerous rocks that they had to climb. They made it to the lake in 10 minutes.

Suddenly, a large beautiful bird appeared from behind the reeds. It was a regal animal and it swam smoothly towards them. The ducklings all squeaked at the same time and picked up the pace. That big beautiful bird was their mother.

The ducklings squawked in happiness and waddled in their mother's direction. When they reached the lake they all dove into the water. They surrounded the mother who made soothing sounds and nuzzled each of them gently with her beak. After a joyous reunion the mother duck and her ducklings turned and started swimming off. Soon they all disappeared behind the swaying reeds, quacking and frolicking with joy.

From that day on Charlie, the Guardian of the Ducks, became famous. He became the superhero of the town. Even the local newspaper published articles about the mysterious hero. And best of all, Charlie knew that no matter what trouble he encountered, his parents would always be there to help him. They were the best sidekicks a superhero could ask for.

Lisa
The Protector of the Weak

Lisa was an angel walking on earth. She had beautiful blonde hair down to her shoulders and bright blue eyes. If someone looked into them, they could hear the soft roar of the endless ocean. Despite her age of only 4 years, she often behaved as a small adult. It was her habit to cheer up her family members and friends. She hated to see anyone feeling sad.

On a day in March, her father's workplace held a *"Bring your child to work day."* Every parent and grandparent could bring their children and grandchildren to work for the entire day. Lisa had been waiting for this day with so much excitement that she could barely contain herself.

Her mother realized how important the event was to her and allowed her to go in her pink superhero costume. The items that made up her costume were her favorite clothes and Lisa always felt super strong when she put them on. Lisa's father shared her love of superheroes, and so when he saw Lisa's outfit for the day he laughed and clapped his hands. Lisa was ready!

The day got off to a good start. When Lisa and her father arrived in the workplace, they were greeted by a delicious stack of steaming hot croissants towering in the company kitchen, along with hot cocoa that had been made for all the little ones. Lisa was happy to start the day with a full belly. On top of that, everyone – both the employees and the other children – really liked her superhero costume. Lisa and the other kids all played together until early afternoon.

They were running around, playing hide and seek, and laughing the entire time. It was the most fun she had ever had!

But then around 2 o'clock in the afternoon, something strange happened. Lisa looked up from her fun and games and saw an older woman running towards the ladies' bathroom. The older woman was wiping her eyes. It looked to Lisa as if she was crying. Lisa, who was very sensitive and caring, would always become alarmed whenever someone was crying. It was her instinct to help whoever was in distress. So, she jumped from her play and went after the older woman.

As Lisa entered the bathroom, she didn't see anyone at first. It seemed as if the lady had suddenly disappeared. But Lisa could hear the sound of someone softly sobbing. She crouched down and peered into the stalls, to see if she could see the old woman's legs.

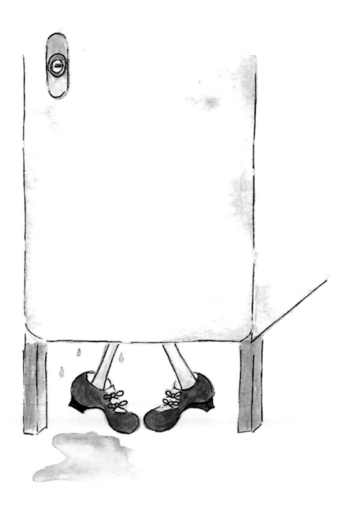

"Hi! I'm the Protector of the Weak! Why are you crying?" Lisa asked in a friendly tone.

Suddenly the sobbing stopped, and the bathroom became silent.
"You can tell me!" Lisa called out. "Don't be scared. It's only the two of us here. You don't have to worry about anything!" Lisa continued in a soft voice.

"They really hurt me," a timid voice explained.

Lisa knew that the timid voice belonged to the old woman. The old woman continued. "Unfortunately, adults sometimes can be very evil. My boss said in front of everyone that I talk too much. Even my small grandchild heard all of it. That is why I went into the bathroom crying." The old lady said this and sniffed back another sob.

"You talk a lot?" asked Lisa, the Protector of the Weak. She didn't know why this would be an insult.

"You know, the problem is, my boss loves to show others that he's the boss and he doesn't care if he hurts someone. And unfortunately, it's easy to hurt me, because I don't ever talk back."

"You know what my parents always say?" asked Lisa.

"No, what?"

"They always say that I shouldn't put myself down. Mean people will try to change the way we think about ourselves, and that is not ok. We have to be strong! So, if your boss is being mean, tell him to stop. Don't let him keep being mean to you." Lisa said.

A great sigh could be heard from the stall, followed by a light chuckle.
"Thank you, sweetheart! I surely needed to hear that. By the way, what's your name?" The old lady asked.

"I'm the Protector of the Weak! But I cannot tell you my real name, because superheroes cannot reveal who they are. Now I'll be going. Be strong and show your grandchildren who's the Super Granny!" Lisa made this declaration and then headed towards the door.

19

"Thank you! You little wonderworker!"

After barely half an hour, everyone was at their desks with their children and grandchildren, working diligently. Lisa was getting to help her father.

Suddenly a short balding gentleman appeared, and he went to the old lady, who was seated nearby, and began to berate her.

"Did you cry enough, Maria? You could show a better example to your grandchild." His mean voice boomed throughout the room.

Then the old lady stood up, straightened herself and said the following:

"Why do you enjoy hurting others? Your life must be pretty sad to enjoy making other people suffer!" she shouted.

"I'm not hurting anyone, I just tell my opinion," the balding boss said.

"You don't think your opinion is hurtful? Do you think it is nice to treat me poorly in front of my grandchildren? No sir, that is not nice at all."

By this time, the whole office was watching them. The balding gentleman's head started getting red and he continued in a stuttering voice.

"Y-y-you don't tal-ta-talk back to me! I'm the boss. And you had-d-d better re-re-respect that!"

This was when the miracle happened. Lisa's father stood up and he said this:

"And you respect others as well!" her father said.

"Yes! I agree!" another gentleman stood up.

"Yes!" said a lady.

"Yes! Yes! Yes!" people stood up one after the other.

The boss couldn't utter a word. He was just staring in front of him. After a moment in which he turned as red as a tomato he simply stormed out of the office.

The little girl hugged the older woman and pride filled her heart.

"I love you, Granny! You're my Super Granny!" The small child said.

Since then, the old lady still sings praises to her coworkers about the mysterious Protector of the Weak and Lisa smiles every time her father tells the story.

Abigail
The Captain of the Flowers

The wind was blowing hard as the children were playing in the garden. Abigail's cousins were visiting from the big city, but she didn't want to play with them. Her cousins' idea of playing was hitting and fighting each other. Abigail wondered if they were so rowdy because they came from the city. The city was full of big cars, bunches of people, and the smell of the streets. Here in the mountains, where Abigail lived, it was the opposite. She lived where the grass was green all year, where the sheep and the cows can come and look inside your windows. Her backyard was a forest. Whenever her cousins came they would run into the forest and start hitting the trees with sticks. She didn't like playing like that. When Abigail went outside she wanted to water the flowers and tend to her little garden. She knew flowers were very important for the environment. It was something her mother had taught her long ago. Ever since her mother had mentioned this she planned to protect the flowers forever. The bumblebees needed the flowers for honey, the women needed them for bouquets, and the world needed them because the flowers were so pretty to look at and smelled so nice.

Whenever the wind would blow hard she would stand in front of the small flower patch and block the wind from knocking them down. When it would rain too much she would hide the flowers under her umbrella to keep them from drowning. She did everything she could to protect them.

As a result of her efforts, Abigail's flowers were the biggest and the brightest in the entire town. Everyone loved to come see the beautiful flowers in her small flower patch. That was why today was the worst day in her life. Her big scary cousin was as mean as he could be. He did not like looking at the flowers. When Abigail turned away she heard a stomping sound behind her.

"Look! I squished a flower!" Her mean cousin laughed.

"NO!" Abigail ran to the flower. Its petals had fallen, and it was no longer bright with color.

"What did you do?" she cried.

Instead of waiting for a response, Abigail ran inside and rummaged through her things. She had a small blanket with bright colored flowers on them. She tied it around her neck so that it looked like a cape. She went back outside and crafted a small headband with leaves and sticks. With the small little pedals that had fallen to the ground, she placed them on her tiara. Then she ran back outside and stood before her cousin.

"I am Abigail. The Captain of the Flowers. You will not hurt any more of my precious flowers." She said these words in a defiant tone, staring up at her big, mean cousin.

Her cousin laughed at her, but Abigail didn't care. She walked around the flower patch for the rest of the day. She watered them carefully and helped the bees find them. Abigail loved every flower. She loved the tall bright sunflowers, the small little daisies, the tulips, and the daffodils. She even loved the dandelions. She would protect them all! After all, that was her vow.

Suddenly, she heard someone coming towards her. She turned around and screamed. Her cousin was walking towards her, carrying a big silver shovel in his hand.

"Why do you like the flowers so much? I don't think they are important. I think we should crush them!" Her cousin came towards her.

"They help us breathe! They give us honey, they help make the world pretty, and they cannot hurt you. So why would you hurt the flowers?" she asked.

"I don't know. Because I want to!" He said and started towards the flowers.

Luckily, Abigail had a plan. She let out a loud whistle that stopped her cousin in his tracks.

"I am not the only one who loves the flowers," Abigail declared. "Say hello to my team of protectors!"

There was a sound that started out as a low humming. It was quiet at first and her cousin looked more confused than scared.

Soon the humming grew louder, and louder, and suddenly it was so loud it sounded like thunder coming towards them. The buzzing bees arrived behind her. Just like Abigail, they were ready to protect the flowers.

Abigail's cousin suddenly looked worried.

"I-I- I am sorry. Ok. Ok. I won't hurt them. I am sorry." Her mean cousin said and ran inside the house.

"YAY!" Abigail cheered.

She thanked her bumblebee friends. The bumblebees buzzed in recognition and then buzzed away back to their hive. It had been an important day for both Abigail and her cousin.

She learned that she truly was the Captain of the Flowers. And her cousin learned that no matter how big or small things may be, when they work together they can be as big as thunder.

Peter
The Super School Boy

Peter didn't know anyone who liked going to school. For that matter, Peter himself didn't like going to school. He didn't like homework, or sitting in class all day, or listening to his teachers. He didn't even like the lunches.

The worst thing of all though, was that Peter wore glasses. He was teased and made fun of for his big glasses because they kept sliding down to the end of his nose. The other kids would point and laugh and call him names.

Sometimes Peter would pretend to be sick just, so he could stay home all day. This morning, however, Peter had a big math test. Despite not liking school Peter actually loved math. But he didn't want to be teased at school and was thinking of how he could get out of going that day.

His mother came into his room that morning and asked him to get ready, but he didn't want to go.

"I can't go. The kids will laugh at me," he said, crossing his arms.

"No one will laugh. And if they do it is because they do not understand you. You will have to teach them. That is what school is for. To help you learn and grow!" his mother said.

"But the kids at school are mean. How will they learn to like me?" Peter asked.

"Just be yourself. Be helpful and good on the inside, and eventually people will see how super you really are," his mother said.

That got Peter thinking. Superheroes often have hidden identities. What if Peter went to school as a superhero? Then no one would know it was him! They would treat him nicely. After all, no one would laugh at a superhero wearing glasses! He knew this plan would work.

He went into his dresser and pulled out an old costume. It was a red suit with a black cape. He pulled out his old homework and taped it onto the costume. He taped a pencil, a paper, an eraser, and even a piece of chalk onto the red suit. The last touch he added was a small little mask underneath his glasses. Now no one would know it was him. To them, he would be known as Super School Boy! Peter put on the outfit and went downstairs to show his mother.

"Wow! Who...Who are you!" she asked.

His plan must be working. Even his own mother didn't recognize him.

"I am Super School Boy!" he said standing tall.

Arriving at school, Peter saw the faces of his classmates staring at him. At first, he was a little bit nervous. But then he remembered that no one knew who he was. He walked into class and sat down at a table. The math test was scheduled for that period.

"Oh no! I hate math." A girl who was sitting next to him said in exasperation. "I just don't understand it!"

"This is a job for Super School Boy!" Peter said boldly, his identity concealed by his mask and superhero outfit. "I can help you understand!"
He explained to the girl about addition, and subtraction, and how someone can do math problems in his or her head. The girl finally began to understand just as the test was being passed out.

"Thank you, Super School Boy!" she said smiling.

It worked! Peter had gone all morning without being teased or called names. And the whole time he was wearing his glasses! He even got to help a student in his class understand math. This was a great day if ever there was one! After the math test Peter went into the lunch room and started eating.

"Hey, superhero," a voice said. It was a scary sounding voice indeed.

"Wha...what?" Peter tried to sound tough.

A bully was walking towards him. Peter watched the bully push another kid to the ground.

"HEY!" Peter said and ran towards the boy on the floor.

"Are you alright? Don't worry. I will protect you." Peter said and helped the boy back up.

The bully looked at Peter. His face was angry and red. He clenched his fists tightly and got ready to hit Peter.

"STOP!" Peter yelled and put his hand out in front of him.

"You can't bully us anymore! It doesn't matter if you are

bigger, or we are smaller. If we are skinny or big, or even if we wear glasses. You can't hurt us anymore!" Peter shouted. When he was dressed in his normal clothes, he was always shy and scared. But this Peter - the Super School Boy - was different. He felt strong. He felt confident. That was why he knew he had to stand up to the bully. Looking around the room the bully looked angry still, but the rest of the students were watching them carefully.

"Super School Boy," one girl began chanting.

"Super School Boy." A few other students joined in.

"Super. School. Boy!" More and more students started chanting.

"SUPER SCHOOL BOY! SUPER SCHOOL BOY! SUPER SCHOOL BOY!" The entire cafeteria was shouting and cheering for him. Peter smiled.

This only made the bully even angrier. He pulled up his hands and ripped the mask off of Peter's face.

"NO!" Peter shouted. They were going to see who he truly was! This was horrible, so horrible indeed.

GASP!

The cafeteria was silent as they looked at Peter in the Super School Boy costume. No one said anything, and the bully was just about to push him to the ground when something incredible happened.

"Peter. Peter. Peter." the kids started saying.

"Peter. Peter! PETER!" They yelled it louder.

They were cheering for him! They were cheering for Peter, the Super School Boy! They did not care that he wore glasses, or that he was really good at math.

They had learned how his heart was on the inside, and that was all that mattered. They were cheering for Peter and the bully gave up and walked away. It was a wonderful day, and the rest of the school year was much easier. Peter made friends and was the Super School Boy who protected the students and helped them with math. He never had to worry about hiding who he was again.

Hannah
The Rescuer of the Sea

Hannah lived on the beach. Her house was only a few short steps from where the waves rolled in. And when it stormed, it seemed as if the sea might come right inside her house, although luckily that never happened.

Hannah loved the ocean and the smell of the sea. She would pretend she was a mermaid and imagine having swimming races with her mermaid friends. The beach that Hannah and her family lived on was very popular. People would come from all over the world just to walk the beach and to swim in the beautiful sea. She met people from Peru, from Germany, and even from Taiwan and New Zealand. So, there were always a lot of new people. The only complaint Hannah had about all the people who visited her beach was that they always brought garbage with them. She didn't like that the people would leave their garbage behind. Because then the garbage would get caught in the sand or sucked out to sea. Sometimes when she was swimming her foot would get caught on a plastic bag and she would lose the mermaid race.

Today when Hannah and her best friend arrived at the beach, they were shocked with what they saw. Standing in the sand was an ugly sign that read:
BEACH CLOSED.

"The beach is closed?! What happened?" Hannah shouted.

That was when she looked across the beach. There were plastic bags, soda bottles, and broken toys all over the sand. There was so much garbage, it was impossible to walk on!

"What are we going to do?" Hannah cried out. "We can't swim. We can't play. We can't even enjoy the sun!" She was very upset.

That was when she saw something in the sand. Her eyes lit up wide. It looked like it was dancing in the wind. She ran over to the object. It was a headband. She pulled it from the sand and wrapped it around her head. The next thing she did was find a long stick from the sea. On the top of the stick she placed a seashell and stood in the sand.

"I am Hannah! The Rescuer of the Sea!" she yelled to the wind.

She started picking up the garbage piece by piece. Hannah had learned how dangerous plastic is for the animals and the water. Just because humans knew how to use the plastic, that didn't mean that the animals did. Some of the birds were flying around with soda cups on their heads, while some starfish were stuck inside an old plastic box.

Hannah carefully helped the animals out of the garbage and tried to teach them about the safety of it.

Then she carefully walked and looked for sharp pieces, and her best friend brought them gloves to keep their hands clean. It was a lot of hard work. There was so much to do, and the sun was beginning to go down. Hannah couldn't wait another day to clean the beach. They had to finish today! There had to be something that the Rescuer of the Sea could do to help!

"Oh no. We will never finish cleaning the beach!" Hannah sounded scared.

Just when things seemed hopeless she had another idea. She ran down the streets to the houses and the stores.

"Hey everybody! We need to clean up the beach! We have to rescue the sea! Come with me! Come with me!" she shouted and danced.

People started looking out from their windows and eventually they came outside and started walking towards the beach. They grabbed trash bags and gloves. There were garbage tins and other things ready to clean up the sand. It was working!

Hannah continued to gather up the people from the town. She told them what the beach looked like. She told them that the sand was in trouble and that the birds were eating bad things. The fish would not swim close to the shore, and the people could no longer sit in the sun. Everyone was shocked! They did not know how badly they were treating the beach. With the Rescuer of the Sea to help them, they were ready to help. Soon others began appearing. And then even more people showed up after that. Everyone was on the beach cleaning the sand, the rocks, the seaweed, and the water. Soon they had collected all the garbage that was around them. Stepping back Hannah took a long look at the scene. It was her beautiful beach again.

"The beach is open again!" a man shouted as he took down the *Closed* sign.

"YAY!" Hannah and the town cheered loudly.

They ran onto the sand and felt the sunset warm their faces. From that day on, Hannah the Rescuer of the Sea would always appear when things began getting messy.
She showed the visitors how to recycle, reuse, and throw things away properly. The sea was protected, and she could swim safely in the water. And she knew the beach would never close again.

Steven
The Hero of the Lost Toys

Steven loved to play pretend. He and his dog Biscuit went on imaginary adventures every single day. Sometimes he would pretend he was flying a plane on the couch, or that he was swimming in a big river when he was in the bathtub. Steven had a big imagination and could make up anything he wanted. But for all the things that he pretended to be, his favorite thing to be was a superhero. He loved being able to help and save people.

But of course, pretending to be a superhero is a lot easier when you have a superhero outfit. And so, whenever Steven played he put on a little yellow cape, a blue t-shirt that went well with the cape, and a little blue mask that went with the t-shirt. But his favorite part of his superhero outfit was the lightning bolts attached to his shoes.

He wore this outfit whenever he played 'superhero,' which was often. That is why Steven was surprised when he discovered his superhero outfit missing.

Well, it wasn't missing exactly. It was just that he couldn't remember where he had left. Steven was about to give up hope when Biscuit started barking. The dog ran into the living room and put its nose under the couch. It continued to bark excitedly until Stephen ran into the room.

"What are you barking at, Biscuit?" he said, slightly annoyed. Biscuit barked randomly sometimes, and this seemed to be a case of that.

Biscuit kept barking and Steven was about to walk back out of the room, when he thought he should probably kneel down and look under the couch. There it was! His superhero outfit! Biscuit had managed to find it. Steven made a note never to doubt Biscuit's bloodhound abilities again.

Steven thanked Biscuit and went to change into his outfit. Once he was dressed up, he went out to play. He was having a great time when he suddenly heard a terrible scream. He looked across the street and saw a little girl crying her heart out. Steven looked at Biscuit. The dog wagged its tail in a frenzy.

"This looks like a job for the Hero of Lost Toys!" Steven said.

Since he was already wearing his superhero outfit, which gave him a sense of purpose, he raced across the street after looking both ways. He ran right up to the little girl.
"What is it? Why are you crying?" Steven asked, standing tall.

"M-M-My Teddy! My Teddy bear is gone!" The girl sobbed.

"Oh. Um. Well. Where did you see it last?" Steven asked.

He had never found a lost toy before, and he didn't even know where to start looking. Even so, he was going to try! He could not give up!

"It was in my backpack. But it's not there anymore." The little girl said.

Steven looked at Biscuit and they nodded to each other. Steven grabbed the backpack and let his dog sniff it with his nose. Biscuit picked up the scent and then he was off! Steven ran closely behind him. They ran down the street, across the road, past a few ice cream stops, and into a small park. Biscuit started sniffing everywhere now, so Steven knew it must be close. He looked everywhere in the grass. There was a playground too and he looked up the slide, down the slide, under the climbing bars, and inside the tunnels. There was no Teddy Bear.

"Come on! We have to keep looking!" Steven said jumping into the sand.

Suddenly Biscuit started barking. Just then he saw a fuzzy little car sticking out of the sand.

He dusted it off with his hand and was able to glimpse the rest. It was the Teddy Bear! He pulled it from the pile and shook out its fur to get it clean. He held the toy in the air and ran back past the park, the ice cream stops, across the road, and up the street. The little girl still waited for them. Her eyes grew wide with excitement and she hugged them both tightly.

"Oh, thank you! Thank you so much - Um. What do I call you?" she asked.

"I am Steven! The Hero of the Lost Toys!" he said proudly.

The girl kissed the dog on the nose and gave Steven one last 'thank you' hug. Steven felt great! It was an amazing feeling to help others. He was just about to walk home when he saw two little boys running towards him.

"Wait! Can you help us? Please! We lost our bike!" they asked him.
Steven looked at his sidekick Biscuit and smiled. They both nodded their heads and ran towards the boys.

"Tell us where you last saw the bike! We will find it!" Steven said with his hands on his hips.

The boys jumped and cheered and started telling Steven and Biscuit where they had last seen the bike. Steven knew he was going to have yet another amazing adventure. All it took was a little hard work, and never giving up. When things got hard, and there was nothing to find sometimes, it was ok. As long as they kept looking and used teamwork to find the lost toys they would always succeed. Steven, the Hero of the Lost Toys would help all of the children in his neighborhood, and even some adults. Soon the city knew that if something was lost, it wouldn't be missing for long. Not when Steven and Biscuit would come to the rescue.

Alix
The Master of Mice

If there was one thing our friend Alix loved more than anything, it was getting to climb in the attic. The attic was full of her parents' old stuff, her grandparents' old stuff, and even her great-great grandparents' stuff. There was always something hidden inside the boxes or dressers that Alix could play with. One time she found a superhero outfit that was purple and green, which were her favorite colors. She would wear the outfit every time she went up into the attic. That was because sometimes it was dark and scary, but when she wore the superhero outfit, she wasn't afraid.

One day Alix was exploring the attic in her superhero outfit when she came across a box in a corner that she hadn't yet explored. She had never seen the box before. It was covered in dust and said *Do Not Open*. Alix walked around the box and looked at it carefully. It was a little box and didn't look at all dangerous.

She really wanted to open it, but the warning made her think twice. She didn't want to get in trouble.

While Alix decided what to do about the box she took a look around the attic. While she was looking around she found a long walking cane. It had a purple handle that matched her outfit perfectly! She held the cane in her hand and poked the small box. Suddenly, something incredible happened. The box moved! It wiggled and bounced and then went back to sitting still. Alix poked the box again. It wiggled and moved again. Her eyes grew wide as her excitement grew. She really wanted to know what was in the box now. What if it was alive? She wondered. What if it was stuck there just waiting to be free?

She poked the box one last time and suddenly it opened. Alix screamed. Mice were running from the box, all over the room. There were so many of them. She counted them as they ran past.
There were almost fifteen!

They were running around the attic in the dressers and the open boxes. They all seemed scared and frightened, looking for someplace to hide. Looking at the small box they came from, she had yet another discovery. There were little blankets and crumbs of cookie and pie from the kitchen inside.

"Oh no! That was your home!" she said to the mice.

Alix knew then she had to do something. The mice were all separated, and they were so scared. Alix went and picked up the small box and sat it in the middle of the room. None of the mice seemed to want to go back in.

"I know! I'll find you all a new box!" Alix promised to the little creatures.

She searched through the attic, looking for the perfect box where they would be safe and sound. She found a thick box sitting on a dresser. It had a small little hole at the bottom of the box, and it looked like the perfect mouse doorway! She took it from the dresser and placed it on the floor. Now she needed to find things that would keep the mice warm. She started dancing around the room with her cane, picking up clothes and old blankets that hadn't been used. As she placed the small blankets in the box, the small mice heads began poking out and looking at her from their hiding places.

"It's ok. Don't be scared," she whispered to them.

They poked out their heads a little further, and she knew they were beginning to trust her. She stepped back from the box and waited for the mice to come into their new home. Some of the mice jumped out from where they were hiding and walked over towards the new box. They sniffed the box a few times, and then scurried away again.
"Wait! What is wrong?" Alix thought.

She had found them the perfect box and added new blankets to keep them warm. Then she remembered. They were probably hungry.

"Stay right there, mice." She said and ran down from the attic.

Running into the kitchen she looked all around, her father was baking a blueberry pie. It smelled delicious and she couldn't wait to eat it for dinner. Her mother was making yummy sandwiches for lunch.
Alix looked around to see what she could bring to the mice.

"Mom? If I were a...a mouse, what would I want to eat?" she asked.

Her mother looked at her with a suspicious smile, and then went to the fridge.

"I suppose if I were a mouse, I would want cheese." Her mother said pulling out a few small slices of cheese.

Her father reached up to the highest part of the cupboard and grabbed a small bag of crackers.

"And if I were a mouse, I would want crackers," her father said and handed her the crackers.

"Thank you so much!" Alix said and ran off.

"Where are you going?" her father asked.

"Umm…to feed the mice, of course!" Alix called out as she ran.

She ran back up into the attic with her hands full of delicious mice food. She placed the food into the box and walked a few more steps back. As soon as the cheesy smell reached the noses of the little mice they were bouncing out of hiding and racing into the box.

"It worked!" she said happily.

Alix stepped closer and closer until she was finally looking into the box. The mice looked up at her, but they no longer seemed scared. They almost looked as if they were smiling.

"I am Alix, the Master of Mice!" she shouted and waved her matching cane in the air.

Every day after that, she would bring up a small piece of cheese and some crackers and have adventures with her little friends. She even trained some of them to jump and to sit. Alix was never scared of the attic again. After all, there was nothing up there to be afraid of. Not even the mice.

Ethan
The Powerful Bugboy

If there was one thing that Ethan loved more than chocolate cake and cotton candy, it was bugs. Not to eat, of course, but to play with, and to protect. He loved watching ants and how they worked so hard to keep their colony safe. He liked playing with grasshoppers and getting into a jumping race with them, even if he always lost. He even loved playing with the spiders. He would find them safe spots to build their webs so that they didn't scare his little sister. It didn't matter what kind of bugs he encountered. Ethan loved them all.

One day he saw a caterpillar moving rather slow on a stick. It looked tired and ill.

Ethan didn't know what to do. He knew from his lessons that caterpillars that were walking on long sticks alone were probably getting ready to turn into a butterfly. It was a really dangerous process because anything could happen while they were in their cocoon! The wind could blow too hard, a hungry bird could swoop down and eat them, and Ethan's baby sister could throw her doll too high in the air.

"No no no, Mr. Caterpillar, you can't stay there! My sister might accidentally hurt you! She's just started walking, she won't under-stand." Ethan said to the slow-moving caterpillar. The caterpillar looked up at him with sad eyes. It was running out of time. They would have to find a place for him to go soon. Ethan wasn't worried. He put the caterpillar in his hands and safely carried him away. He was Ethan, the Powerful Bugboy!

He had a long black cape that went down to his ankles. And he wore a bright yellow shirt so that bees would know he was friendly. On the top of his head he did not wear a mask, or a crown, or even a hat. He wore antennas! They were made from springs and cotton balls that he had glued together himself. These little touches helped the insects know that they could trust him.

With his Bugboy suit on Ethan got ready to look for a safe place for the caterpillar. He ran to one side of his yard. The ants were gathering food and he could see there was a tree just above the ant hill.

"This looks like a safe place," he said to the caterpillar.

Just as he was about to place the bug on a branch he saw the ants begin to dance and squeak. Looking at all the ants they started moving and it looked as if they were spelling out something. *NO*. The ants made the letters with their bodies.

"But why?" he asked.

Just then he looked around the tree and saw a fuzzy ball of fur hiding in the shade. It was long and black with claws as sharp as knives.

"Oh. I see. No, no, Mr. Caterpillar. You *definitely* can't stay here. That is our cat's sleeping spot." Ethan said and went on looking again.

The caterpillar looked even weaker now. Luckily, Ethan, the Powerful Bugboy was on the case! He went to the other side of the yard and saw a small spot where a cocoon would fit nicely. The crickets and grasshoppers began squeaking their hind legs and warning Ethan that it was not the best place. That was when he saw the sprinkler hose right next to him on the grass.

"Oh no. Dad waters the grass a lot, we can't put you here." Ethan said.
So, Ethan searched even more. He climbed under the porch, up into the trees, and even onto his swing set. Then he had an idea. He ran into his front yard and saw a big bushy rose bush. Slipping the caterpillar inside, he finally breathed a sigh of relief.

"This is the perfect place. My sister can't come out to the front yard, the birds don't like the thorns, and the big bush will protect you from the wind!" Ethan said reassuringly.

The caterpillar smiled brightly and started building its cocoon. The fuzzy bug looked like a little child pulling a blanket around itself to keep warm. Ethan was proud, and through the next week he watched and protected the caterpillar. He knew that the next time he saw the bug it would look very different. It would be a colorful creature with beautiful wings and knowing this gave Ethan a special feeling. In his own way, he was helping to make the future a more beautiful place. All in all, it was another successful job for Ethan, the Powerful Bugboy.

Tiana
The Savior from the Storms

Pop! Pop! Drop! Drip! The rain was falling down hard onto the roof. Tiana could hear how loud each rain drop sounded.

"AHH!!!" The children in the room screamed. All of them except Tiana.

They were in a great big house full of people that her mother and father worked with. There were big kids and small kids and even some babies. Tiana was upset that she was put into the children's room at first. But that was before she knew she would save the day. A sudden bolt of lightning flashed, and thunder boomed around them.

"AHH!!" The children screamed again. A baby started crying.

It was an important night for Tiana's parents, and they let her pick out her own outfit. She decided to choose a superhero suit that was all the colors of the rainbow. She had bright red socks, purple flower pants, an orange shirt, green cloves, a yellow cape, and a blue mask. Though everyone knew that she was Tiana, they didn't know how strong she really was. They didn't know that she was a superhero for real.
The thunder sounded again and the children all screamed.

"I want my mommy!" a little boy cried.

"I want to go home!" another child wailed.

"I'm scared!" a little girl whimpered.

"Don't worry! Tiana, the Savior from the Storms, is here to help you." Tiana said, letting her voice boom out to match the thunder.

The children all looked at her with confused faces. They were huddled up tight underneath a blanket. Tiana had to find a way to help the kids feel safe again. She used the stories her mother would tell her, and how she learned not to be afraid of storms.

"You can't be afraid of thunder! It's...it's just the rain cloud men... Dancing! You know?" Tiana said.

"Is it really?" a boy asked.

"Let's play pretend!" Tiana said excitedly. "The rain cloud men are tall. Their arms are blue, and they love dancing to disco! So, what we are going to do? We are going to play some music and dance! Now, every time the thunder comes, we have to freeze in our favorite dance position!" Tiana said, showing her dance moves.

Some of the children smiled. And then the lightning flashed, and they screamed again.

"What do we do for that?" A girl hid under the covers.

"We…We cheer really loud! That means we… we out-danced the rain cloud men! We won! It's a dance competition!" Tiana said.

The children all seemed to like the idea. Tiana found some music and flung her cape in the air. She helped the children out from under the blankets and got them all in position to dance. Even if she was still a little afraid of the thunder storm, she would be brave.
That was what superheroes do.

"Ok. Now dance!" Tiana started the music and the kids all danced.

Tiana danced with her arms and shook her head to the beat. As they were all beginning to laugh the thunder came. The kids started to scream but Tiana shouted first.
"Freeze! Hold still! The lighting will tell us if we won!" Tiana froze.

The rest of the children stopped dancing and stood still as the thunder passed. A few minutes later a flash of lightning appeared.

"YAY!" The children yelled. They were winning the dance competition against the rain cloud men.

"This is so much fun!" A boy said as he started dancing again.

Tiana in her rainbow super suit danced across the couch. The kids followed behind her and they all danced away their fear. They were no longer scared of the thunder and the lightning. When the thunder *BOOMED*, they would stand still and freeze. When the lightning would flash, they would cheer and keep dancing. Tiana was smiling as she saw the children having fun again. Even the babies were clapping and smiling and bouncing in their places. The children danced and danced until the parents came to get them.

"Wow, what happened here?" Tiana's mother asked as she saw all the children dancing.

"We are dancing with the rain cloud men." Tiana said smiling.

"I see." Her mother said and picked her up.

"Thank you, Tiana!" the children all yelled.

"You are welcome!" she said back.

The next time a thunder or lightning storm happened all the kids knew that they would never be scared again. As long as they practiced their dance moves from time to time, they would be just fine. As for Tiana, the Savior from the Storms, it was just the beginning of a long and illustrious career of saving kids from storms.

THE END

Made in the USA
Middletown, DE
03 January 2019